# Princess Parade

Adapted by Samantha Brooke from the script by Corey Powell

SCHOLASTIC INC.

ISBN 978-0-545-58126-4

©2013 MGA Entertainment, Inc. and Viacom International Inc.
All Rights Reserved.
LALALOOPSY™ and all pre-existing underlying, names, characters, likenesses, images, related titles and logos are trademarks of MGA Entertainment, Inc. in the U.S. and other countries. Nickelodeon and all related titles and logos are trademarks of Viacom International Inc.

12 11 10 9 8 7 6 5 4 3 2 1                                      13 14 15 16 17 18/0

Designed by Angela Jun and Two Red Shoes Design
Printed in the U.S.A.
First printing, September 2013                                        40

"I am honored to be president of the Princess Club!" said Jewel Sparkles. "Tippy Tumblelina, I crown you vice president!"

"This is *tutu* exciting!" cried Tippy, wobbling a bit.

"My tiaras are all so beautiful," said Jewel. "I wish we had more princesses to show them off."

utside, Jewel and Tippy saw Peanut Big Top, Spot Splatter Splash, and Sunny Side Up. They were fixing Sunny's wagon. "I want you all to join our Princess Club," said Jewel. "I never saw myself as a princess. But sure, why not?" said Spot.

"Count me in!" cried Peanut.

"Sorry, Jewel. I have to fix my wagon," said Sunny.

"Pretty please, with sparkles on top?" Jewel asked.

"I guess I can be a princess for a little while," said Sunny.

"I will teach you to be a princess in three lessons!" Jewel said. She gave each girl a tiara. "Lesson one: walking like a princess." Tippy showed them how to walk gracefully across the room. But she didn't notice her ballet slippers were untied.

"*Whoops!*" Tippy cried as she slid across the floor.

"That looks like fun!" cried Sunny. She slid across the floor just like Tippy.

"How was that?" Sunny asked Jewel.

"Not quite right," answered Jewel. "Let's move on, shall we?"

"Lesson two: talking like a princess," said Jewel. "Tippy will serve tea. Listen to how we speak."

"How many sugar cubes would you like, Your Royal Highness?" asked Tippy.

"I will have two cubes, thank you," answered Jewel. "Now you try."

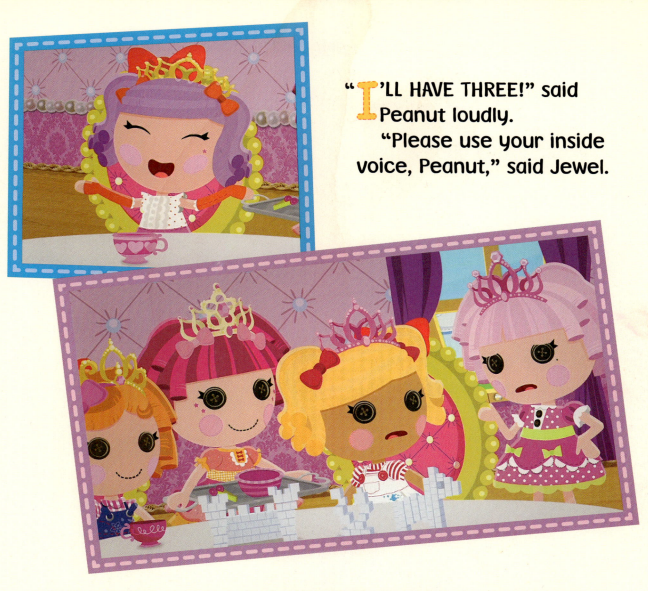

"**I**'LL HAVE THREE!" said Peanut loudly.

"Please use your inside voice, Peanut," said Jewel.

"I'll have them all!" cried Spot. She used the sugar cubes to make sculptures.

Jewel shook her head. "Sugar cubes aren't art supplies. They're for putting in tea. We'll have to work on that."

"**L**esson three: dressing like a princess," said Jewel.

Peanut chose a fabulous dress . . . with clown shoes.

Spot wore a sparkly gown with way too much jewelry.

Sunny chose a lovely dress just like Jewel's. But the fabric made her skin itch.

When they went outside, Jewel spotted Sunny's wagon. It gave her an idea. "We should show off our tiaras in a Princess Parade with wagons and floats!"

"I can help decorate," offered Spot.

"No, no," said Jewel. "You all must practice being princesses. I know just the person to help decorate."

Jewel and Tippy went to see Crumbs Sugar Cookie, the best baker in Lalaloopsy Land. They explained their Princess Parade idea.

"Can the decorations be made of food?" asked Crumbs.

"Of course!" Jewel cried.

"Sweet! Let's get started," said Crumbs.

The girls took everything they had baked over to the wagons.

"Now what do we do?" asked Tippy.

Crumbs held up a spatula dripping with pink icing. "We stick it all together with icing!"

"Our tiaras will really shine against all this pink," said Jewel when she stepped back to admire their creation.
Elephant was excited, too. He raced to the front of the floats.
"Thank you, Elephant, but it's too heavy for you to pull," said Jewel.

While the girls went inside for a snack, Elephant tried to pull the floats again. This time he got a little help.

The pets pulled and pulled. Finally, the floats began to move. But soon the floats were moving too fast!

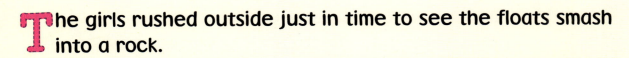

The girls rushed outside just in time to see the floats smash into a rock.

"All of our hard work has been ruined!" cried Jewel. "Now we'll have to call off the parade."

Sunny, Spot, and Peanut heard the commotion. "Maybe it will all be okay. I can fix the wheels that fell off," said Sunny. "With a little frosting . . . and a little luck . . . this should work!"

"**T**here's nothing that icing can't fix!" Spot said. She grabbed frosting tubes and got to work.

Sunny shoveled cake with a fork. "It's just like being on the farm," she said.

Finally, Peanut filled balloons with sprinkles and then let them pop. "Sprinkles away!" she cried. It was raining sprinkles!

"Now these floats are perfectly perfect!" said Jewel. "I can't wait until everyone—"

"Everyone?" asked Tippy.

"Oh, no, I forgot to send invitations!" cried Jewel.

"Don't worry, Jewel, I know just how to fix this problem," said Peanut.

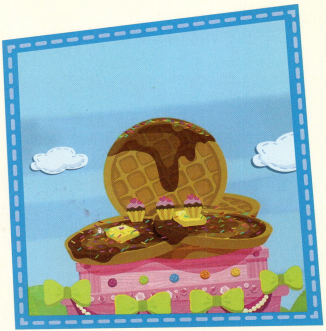

**P**eanut used her loudest outside voice to announce the start of the parade. "Right this way, folks, for the most royal, the most majestic parade in Lalaloopsy Land history!"
Soon everyone had gathered for the parade.

"So, are all my princesses ready?" Jewel asked.

Spot had added some new, artistic touches to her gown.

Tippy was tangled up in tulle and ribbons.

Sunny had hitched up her dress so she could move more easily.

Jewel was worried. "But your costumes are—"
"Splendiferous!" shouted Peanut. "Let's start the parade!"
"You're right!" said Jewel. "There never would have been a Princess Parade without each of you . . . including Elephant!"
He was up front pulling the parade.

"Well, I guess there's more than one way to be a princess!" said Jewel. "And more than one way to pull a parade!"